A BID FOR MURDER

PAINT AND SIP COZY MYSTERIES, BOOK 2

DONNA CLANCY

SUMMER PRESCOTT BOOKS PUBLISHING

Copyright 2024 Summer Prescott Books

All Rights Reserved. No part of this publication nor any of the information herein may be quoted from, nor reproduced, in any form, including but not limited to: printing, scanning, photocopying, or any other printed, digital, or audio formats, without prior express written consent of the copyright holder.

**This book is a work of fiction. Any similarities to persons, living or dead, places of business, or situations past or present, is completely unintentional.

CHAPTER ONE

"Don't forget, ladies. There's no painting class next Thursday night because it's Thanksgiving. Saturday night's arts and crafts class will be at its usual time," Jannelle stated as some of the women were getting ready to leave. "We'll be making pinecone centerpieces for your Christmas tables."

"I'm so glad in just a few short weeks things have returned to normal around here," Anita said, "We are back to our old happy group of artists and wine tasters."

"Even Sally and Kristen are back to being friends," Mollie added. "All the women who were supposed to be seeing Devon weren't even involved with him. He still has his harem, it's just not so large."

"He's young and handsome. Let him have his fun. Someday he'll find the right woman and settle down, until then, it gives us something to gossip about," Jannelle replied.

"Gossip? We don't gossip in here, we trade facts. Now whether those facts are true or not is anyone's guess," Anita said, stifling a smile. "Don't you agree, Mollie?"

"Oh, most definitely."

"Before you leave, can I have a show of hands of who wants to do a Secret Santa?" Jannelle asked.

Everyone raised their hands.

"Awesome! We'll have a Christmas party the Saturday evening before Christmas. Once we draw names you can bring your wrapped gift here in a brown paper bag, so no one knows who brings what and who gives what. I'll have a sign-up sheet next Saturday night," Jannelle stated.

"And don't forget there is a fifteen-dollar limit on the gift," Anita said.

"I'm glad you upped it from the ten-dollar limit you had last year," Sally said. "It wasn't easy finding something nice for that amount of money."

"I don't know, I think the gifts were pretty nice last year," Mollie replied. "I received a beautiful potpourri burner that I use all the time. Not that my husband appreciates the calming smells in the house, mind you."

"I received a cheese board that is used at every class for refreshments," Anita said.

"And surprisingly, no one ever told anyone else who they bought gifts for. It was truly a Secret Santa," Mollie added. "Well, I'm off. I left a dinner in the fridge for my husband but knowing him he came home and fell asleep in his recliner without heating it up and eating. See everyone next Saturday night. Happy Thanksgiving!"

"Happy Thanksgiving! And tell George the same," Jannelle replied.

A short time later, the clean-up was done, and the women were heading home. The next two days the shop was closed. Paint and Sip would be opened Tuesday and Wednesday during the day, each woman taking a shift, and close at five on Wednesday for the Thanksgiving holiday on Thursday.

"Are you sure you won't join us for our Thanksgiving meal?" Anita asked her friend as she locked the shop door.

"No, I'm good, thank you. I ordered a turkey dinner with all the trimmings from the market that's going to be delivered to the house. I'm going to stay home in my pajamas and share my food with Picasso and Petunia."

"Okay, if you change your mind you can let me know next week."

Petunia was waiting at the door, tail wagging wildly, when Jannelle arrived home. Picasso couldn't be bothered to jump down from the bay window to say hello. He stretched, curled up in a ball and closed his eyes again.

"Come on, Petunia. Let's make a quick trip outside and not far from the back porch. I saw a couple of coyotes up the street on the way home," Jannelle said, clipping on the dog's leash.

Minutes later they were back in the house safe and sound, and Petunia was enjoying her supper. Picasso strolled into the kitchen, let out a meow and sat in front of the fridge waiting for his supper.

"You do realize this is the month of the art auction for the shelter?" she said to the cat as she placed his wet food down on the floor. "The Jingle Bell Auction has already been announced and tickets are already being sold for the event. I need you to buckle down and get at least three paintings done."

The cat ignored her and kept eating.

"You haven't produced a single piece of artwork in the last six months. It's time you got off your high horse and cooperated. Your fellow animals are counting on you," she said, popping some leftover chicken alfredo in the microwave.

Jannelle sat at the table waiting for her supper to finish heating up.

"It would be nice if we could get you to create a painting, too, Petunia," Jannelle said, standing up when the buzzer went off. "Let's see, what wine do I want to drink tonight?"

She poured herself a glass of chilled cranberry apple wine and sat down in her recliner to watch some television and eat. Picasso jumped up on the footrest of the recliner and proceeded to clean himself after eating. Petunia wedged her way in between Jannelle's hip and the arm of the chair, let out a loud sigh and fell sleep with a full stomach.

This is the life. I am so glad I decided to retire when I did. Just my animals and me. It doesn't get any better than this.

She finished eating and picked up her book that was next to her chair. It was due back at the library on Monday and she was only halfway done with it. Jannelle couldn't renew it because there was a waiting list for it as it was a new release, and many people wanted to read it. She read for the next two hours, and then gathered up the animals and went upstairs to bed.

The next morning, Jannelle took Petunia for an extra-long walk around the yard. The dog pranced around, happy to be out in the fresh air. Picasso watched from the bay window. Even though it was November, it was warm outside, and they both enjoyed their walk.

They returned inside and Jannelle grabbed a second cup of coffee and finished the last two chapters of the book she was reading the previous night. She closed the book trying to decide what to do next. It was warm outside and there wouldn't be a better day to put out her Christmas lights and not freeze her fingers off while doing it.

She climbed up the attic stairs and grabbed a storage box marked outdoor lights. Petunia was waiting at the bottom of the stairs and insisted on sniffing the box all over before Jannelle could set it up on the kitchen table to open it.

Every year when the lights came down after the holidays, Jannelle made sure she put everything away neatly and orderly so it would be easy to decorate the following year. She didn't want to have to spend hours untangling strings of lights before they could be hung. The nails were left up on the gutters outside so she could follow the same pattern from the year before.

The only things she moved around were the individual items which would make the yard look different year to year. A family of gold reindeer, light-up piles of plastic presents, and several different styles of snowman would be scattered around the yard to make it merry and bright. She hadn't bought any new outside decorations in a few years and decided this year she would look around to buy something to add to the collection displayed in the yard.

"Wouldn't it be funny if I could find a big bottle of wine that lights up?" she asked the dog while she rummaged through the junk drawer searching for the four-way outlet plugs. "Everyone would know it was my house."

Petunia tilted her head, listening but not understanding what was being said. She thought she was going to get a treat out of the open drawer. Realizing what the dog was waiting for, Jannelle opened the adjoining drawer and gave Petunia a treat, who happily retreated to the living room and her bed to eat it.

"Where did I put those outlet plugs last year?" she asked herself, not finding them in the drawer where they usually were stored.

Her cell phone rang as she stood in the middle of the kitchen trying to remember.

"Hello."

She listened to whoever was calling her, and she smiled.

"That is great news. I guess Picasso needs to start painting for the auction. Thanks for letting me know. I'll be there for the meeting. Talk to you later."

Jannelle walked into the living room looking for the cat. He was in his usual spot, sprawled out in the sunshine in the bay window.

"Hey, lazy bones. How about we do some painting today? The Jingle Bell Auction is going to be covered by several of the bigger newspapers around the Cape and they want to feature your paintings. Think about how much more money we can take in for the Denniston Rescue if you just put yourself out there and try to be productive," Jannelle said, scratching the cat behind his ears. "What do you say? Painting after I put up the Christmas lights?"

Picasso opened one eye, looked at his owner, turned over, and went back to sleep.

"You have got to be the laziest cat I know," she said, laughing. "I will be back to get you, and we *will* be painting today. So, rest up while you can."

Jannelle returned to the kitchen determined to find the outdoor plugs. Eventually, she found them in another drawer where she had never stored them before.

"Now, why would I have put these in there?" she asked herself, shaking her head. "Oh, well, on to decorating."

It was a gorgeous day, so Jannelle attached Petunia to her runner and let her get some much-needed exercise. She'd run for a bit and then wander over to the area Jannelle was decorating and watch what her owner was doing.

Jannelle was up on the ladder and happened to drop the string of lights she had coiled on the ladder hook. They landed on top of Petunia who was laying under the ladder, and it scared the daylights out of her. She took off running and didn't stop until she ran out of lead and couldn't go any further.

Jannelle hurried over to the dog, picked her up, and spoke softly to her to calm her down. She decided the dog had had enough fresh air and brought her, along with a treat, to her bed inside and let her take a nap.

She finished stringing the lights that trimmed the house and set to work placing the various snowmen in different corners of the yard. The two piles of plastic presents were placed on either side of the entrance to the driveway. The reindeer family was placed in the center of the area inside the half circle the driveway formed. The extension cords were anchored down into the ground with pieces of rounded wire that Jannelle had designed herself and reused every year.

She looked around, satisfied with her work. Later, she would go online and see if she could find a light-up bottle of wine even if people might look at the decoration as a New Year's one and not Christmas.

Now, we'll be ready to turn on the lights Thanksgiving night.

Jannelle made herself some lunch and ate with two sets of eyes watching her every move. Petunia's eyes traveled from plate to her owner's mouth with every bite her owner took of the roast beef sandwich. Picasso became bored halfway through lunch and disappeared to eat some of his own dry food.

"I love Sundays," she said to Petunia, giving her a small piece of meat out of the sandwich. "No meetings, no classes, and nothing to do but what I chose to do. And after I eat, I choose to take a nap. I do have a meeting today at six o'clock, but it will be a short one."

Rested after a nice, two-hour nap, Jannelle pulled out the folder to go over the auction materials she had collected. She was in charge of the donations and had collected many items over the last month. The highlight and the main draw would be Picasso's paintings. As much as Jannelle didn't understand the fascination with the cat's paintings, she welcomed the interest as her cat made a sizable amount of money for the shelter.

The auction would be held at the Paint and Sip, the second Saturday of December. The doors would open an hour before the actual auction took place so people could come in and peruse the items that were being offered. The auction itself would begin at two o'clock.

Almost every business in town had donated something, from items featured in their shops to gift certificates for people to buy what caught their personal fancy. Denniston and its people always supported the auction well and looked out for the shelter and its animals. Most of the locals' furry family members came from the shelter which took in animals from all over the state to find them new homes. Jannelle had many pets in the past who had come from the shelter and found their way to her house, Picasso and Petunia included.

As she went through the paperwork, she kept count of the number of items she already had in her possession for the auction and the ones that had been promised but not received yet. At the end of her tally, she had thirty-six items already in the back room at the shop with eighteen more on the way.

"It seems we are down under our count from last year. I guess it's time for another email blast to go out to our past sponsors. I understand times are tougher this year, but every little bit helps the shelter."

She gathered up the paperwork and stood up, looking for the cat.

"Picasso! Do you feel artistic today?"

Jannelle put up a gate across the kitchen doorway to keep Petunia out. She laid a large tarp on the floor and set three stretched, framed canvases at different spots on the floor. Using poster paint that cleans up easily with warm water and was nontoxic, she poured little piles of different colored paint around each of the canvases.

"Now for my secret weapon," she said, setting four catnip mice around on the tarp. "Okay, Picasso, do your thing."

She climbed over the gate and sat in the living room, ignoring the cat and the kitchen area. Petunia walked to the gate several times not understanding why she couldn't go into the kitchen.

"Come sit with me, Petunia," she called to the dog.

The dog settled into the chair with her owner, who picked up another book to finish which also had to be returned to the library the following day. A short time later, Picasso jumped the gate into the kitchen and Jannelle could hear the rustling of the tarp.

"It's a good thing Picasso doesn't mind baths," Jannelle said to the dog. "And I don't mind cleaning up pawprints everywhere. It kind of makes my house unique, having cat prints everywhere."

Jannelle read another two chapters and then went to check on the cat. Picasso was laying on his back holding a catnip mouse between his two front paws. Two of the canvases had been walked and rolled on by the cat. Not many of the paint piles had been disturbed, so she let the cat be to see what would happen.

She returned to her chair and didn't leave it until she finished the book. It had gotten quiet in the kitchen.

Jannelle and Petunia stood at the gate, looking for the cat. The tarp had been gathered up in several places and all three canvasses had been 'painted'. Picasso, drunk from the catnip and worn out from playing, had jumped up on one of the kitchen chairs and fallen asleep.

"Well, they are not up to your usual standards, but I guess they will do," Jannelle said, stepping over the gate. "This one is unique."

She picked up one of the canvases. One of the catnip mice Picasso had been playing with was covered in paint and stuck to the painting. She turned it upside down and the mouse stuck where it was.

"I have the perfect frame for this one," Jannelle said to Petunia, who was whining at the gate.

She picked up the other two paintings and set them on the counter. Next, she folded up the canvas being careful not to let the paint get on the floor underneath. Once that was done, she took the gate down and let the dog into the kitchen. The three canvases were moved to the kitchen table where they could dry.

"I know you want to sleep," she said to the cat, picking him up. "But let's get some of the paint off you before it totally dries."

She set the cat in the sink and sprayed warm water all over him. He stretched and stuck his nose up in the air. She rubbed the cat shampoo on him, and he rolled around in the sink as she lathered him up. He wasn't as covered as he usually was, so clean up was done in half the time.

"You are such an awesome cat to be helping your friends at the shelter like you are," Jannelle said, drying the cat with a towel. "Personally, I think you like the warm baths, or you just don't care because of the catnip. I'm not sure which."

Picasso looked up at her with a look of pure love and contentment. He knew he had done a good job. Jannelle took him to the bay window and set him in the warm sun for a well-earned nap. He was asleep in minutes.

"Let's take one more trip outside and then I have to leave for my meeting," she said, attaching the dog's leash to her collar. "I'll give you supper before I leave."

Half an hour later, Jannelle was pulling into the parking lot of the Denniston Community Center. She grabbed her cell, purse, and folder of papers and went inside. Anita and Mollie were enjoying a cup of coffee just inside the door.

"Jannelle, wait until you see the donation Mollie managed to get today for the auction. It's amazing," Anita said. "I think it should be our grand prize for our raffle and not an item in the auction."

"Let me get some coffee and we'll all sit down and start the meeting. Then you can announce it to everyone," Jannelle replied.

She grabbed her coffee along with a piece of homemade apple strudel that Anita had made and brought to the meeting.

"Ladies, shall we get started? Refill your coffee or tea and take a seat, please."

"How are we doing for donations this year?" Sally asked.

"I went over my paperwork today. So far, we have a little over fifty items for the auction. We are a little behind last year's totals, but I did manage to get

Picasso motivated and he got three paintings done today, two for the auction and one for the raffle."

"Speaking of the raffle, my husband picked up the tickets yesterday from the printer. We can pass them out tonight to get started selling them. I'm going to make my way around town tomorrow and give some to each business on Main Street for them to sell to their customers," Mollie stated. "The day after Thanksgiving is a big shopping day so hopefully they'll sell lots of tickets."

"I have three more gift certificates from the salon to add to the total," Sally said, sliding three white envelopes down to Jannelle.

"I know times are tougher this year for lots of people, so let's just do our best to make the Jingle Bell Auction as successful as we can," Anita said. "Our furry friends are depending on us."

"I'll be putting Picasso's paintings in the window of the Paint and Sip on Wednesday, once I have them framed," Jannelle said. "That might drum up a little bit of business for the raffle as people are walking around shopping on Main Street."

"Now, I believe that Mollie has another announcement to be made,' Anita said.

"I have. I've been calling around trying to get donations for either the auction or the raffle. And did I score big," Mollie replied, smiling.

"Well, don't keep us in suspense," Jannelle said.

"Truth be told, it was really my husband who scored big for us," Mollie started. "He called a friend of his over in Yarmouth that owns The Yard Beautiful."

"I've heard of that place, but I've never been there. They build the most beautiful decks and firepits," Sally said. "My ex-father-in-law had his deck built by them and it's beautiful."

"Peter, the owner, had graciously offered to build a deck for the grand prize winner of the raffle. He said he would offer five different decks to pick from and his guys would install it in the spring."

"Wow! I'll buy a whole bunch of the raffle tickets for a chance at a deck on my house," Sally stated. "Why is he offering such a big prize?"

"His dog, Pepper, was having stomach problems. Peter brought him to vet at the rescue and Mary found he had ingested some jacks the kids left on the floor, and they had lodged in his intestines. She operated, removed the jacks, and Pepper is doing great now. He loves his dog, and was so grateful, he wants to help raise money for the rescue."

"That kind of prize is really going to draw in the ticket sales," Jannelle said. "We need to get some flyers printed up stating the deck will be the grand prize and spread them around town."

"I may have to do an extra pick-up of monies before we have our next meeting," Carol Finch, the group's treasurer stated. "I can do a walk through the town on Sunday afternoon, visit the businesses that are selling the raffle tickets, and bring the money here to count that night. I can make a deposit at the night deposit on my way home after the meeting concludes."

"I can make up a flyer and hand them out around town tomorrow afternoon," Fran Dower, the head librarian said. "I just need the details you want on the flyer."

"It sounds like we have a plan. Keep pushing for donations and we'll meet here again next Sunday night," Jannelle said. "Now, it's time for a glass of wine and another strudel."

An hour later, after several glasses of wine and quite a bit of gossip being exchanged, the meeting broke up and everyone headed home. It was dark outside when Jannelle arrived home, and she had forgotten to leave any lights on in the house.

"My poor babies," she muttered, closing and locking her car door. "They've been in the dark all night."

She opened the door and Petunia was there, tail wagging. Picasso sauntered his way out of the living room into the kitchen. He sat down in front of his food dish and looked at his owner like, well, what are you waiting for?

"I'm so sorry I didn't leave the lights on for you guys," Jannelle said, setting down her purse on the kitchen counter. "I forget how early it gets dark now. Let's get you outside to do your business, Petunia, and then Picasso, I'll be back in to feed you."

The animals fed; Jannelle sat down to eat the burger she picked up at a fast-food restaurant on the way home. French fries and onion rings were included in the meal along with a large soda. The cat and dog finished their own meals and sat on either side of their owner waiting for their share of the burger patty.

"Boy, I remember the day I used to be able to eat without so many eyes watching me," she said, giving them each a small piece of meat. "You guys are so lucky I don't mind sharing."

Jannelle didn't like to go to bed right after eating a big meal, but she had a busy schedule for the next day. Sundays and Mondays were her days off as Anita watched the store on Monday and had Sundays and Tuesdays off. There were no classes at night on those three nights and only the retail aspect of the store was open for business.

She tossed her wrappers in the trash, washed her hands to get the grease from the fries and onion rings off, and checked to make sure the doors were locked.

"Let's go, guys. It's time for bed," she said, picking up the dog and shutting off the kitchen light.

CHAPTER TWO

Jannelle was up and out early in the morning. Her first stop was the Denniston Library.

"Good morning, Jannelle," Fran said. "I already have the flyers done if you'd like to take some with you to pass out."

"That was fast," Jannelle replied, setting her books on the counter to return them.

"I had time this morning before the library opened. What do you think?" she asked, handing her a flyer.

"This is great. I love the deck centered in the middle of the flyer. It really makes it pop."

"I thought so. Hopefully, this will bring in more sales on the raffle to make up for the lack of silent auction items," Fran stated, zapping the bar code on the back of each book. "I have the new mystery you were on the waitlist for. Do you want to take it today?"

"I do and I think I'll look around for a couple more books to take with me."

Jannelle walked around the first floor, browsing the books in the stacks. She was always drawn to the mystery section first, but she had read most of the books contained there. Any new mysteries that were being released; she was on the waitlist for.

Her next favorite genre was biographies. She loved history and was fascinated by the people who shaped the country she lived in. Some were good people, and some were serial killers. She read them all.

"I'll take these today," she said to Fran, laying three books on the counter.

"The only one due back in a week is the new mystery," Fran said, adding the book to the pile. "The others are due back in two weeks."

"The library seems to be a new regular stop on my Monday schedule," Jannelle said, smiling. "I'll take a bunch of the flyers as I am stopping several places, including the rescue."

"I can't wait for Mary to see the donation of the deck. She will freak out," Fran stated. "As the only vet in the area, she needs all the help she can get for the running of the rescue and animal hospital."

"She does. I thought you were off on Mondays. You said last night at the meeting you were going to pass out the flyers around town today."

"I usually am, but Cheryl's daughter went into labor early this morning, so I volunteered to cover her shift. I'll be out at three and will take a stroll around town then," Fran replied.

"I'm going to the grocery store, the rescue, and the Wine Depot. I can put flyers there so you can cross those spots off your walk," Jannelle offered.

"Get some good, holiday flavored wines for us to try while we create," Fran requested.

"I will. I'm going to look for some new and different wines we haven't tasted before. And I have to order the wine for the silent auction, both for prizes and for drinking during the event. Any requests?"

"I wasn't a big fan of the cranberry wine even though I know that's a holiday flavor. The Raspberry Crisp wine was really good. Maybe you could get some of that?"

"That's the wine Mollie requested I try to get. The sweet raspberry, with the tartness of the green apple combines well to make a nice tasting wine. As a matter of fact, I liked it so much I think I have a case of it in my wine cellar at the house."

"Well, if you draw my name for Secret Santa, I know what you can get me," Fran hinted.

"But then you'd know who your Secret Santa would be," Jannelle said, laughing.

"No one else would have to know I know. Just saying."

"On that note, I will take my flyers and be on my way," she replied, picking up her books.

"I'll see you Saturday night at class," Fran said. "Have a great Thanksgiving."

Jannelle made a quick stop at the grocery store. She picked up what she needed, verified her order for her Thanksgiving meal delivery, and hung the flyers in the window and on the bulletin board. One of the cashiers said if they made the flyers half the size they were, they could put one in each customer's shopping bag. Jannelle promised to talk to Fran about the suggestion.

The Wine Depot was one of Jannelle's favorite places in town. She was an avid wine drinker and didn't hesitate to try all the various flavors the Wine Depot offered. Sal and Maria Salmeri opened the business over thirty years ago and it seemed like the wines they offered got better and better every year.

Jannelle liked to put aside at least an hour when she visited so she could sample the wines and put together her monthly order. This order was going to be much larger than usual as it was for the month of December for the shop and the Jingle Bell Auction. She brought the store credit card in case she went a little overboard in her ordering, which she usually did.

"My good friend," Sal said, throwing his hands in the air and heading her way to give her a big hug.

"Sal, how are you?"

"I am good, and so is my beautiful bride. You just missed her. She's on her way up to the vineyards to find some new wines for our store. What can I do for you today?"

"First off, can you hang some of these flyers around your store for the Jingle Bell Auction?"

"Tony, take these and hang them in the window and on the door. Tape one next to the register on the counter so people will see it when they check out," Sal instructed his employee.

"Thank you, Sal. The auction is very important to the Denniston Rescue. They count on our donation every year to stay in business," Jannelle said, handing him some flyers.

"Are you here for a donation?"

"Marie already gave us two gift certificates for the store, and we thank you so much for the donation. I am actually here to place an order; a rather large order."

"Those are some of my favorite words," he replied, smiling and taking her arm. "Come, let us go to the tasting room. I have some wonderful new wines for your art students to try."

For the next hour, Jannelle sat tasting the small glasses of wine placed in front of her. She and Sal chatted about anything and everything. She ordered several new flavors for the shop including a Christmas Plum, a new blush, and a brand-new vanilla flavored wine.

The order for the auction was placed next. She ordered two cases that held a variety of wines for prizes and ten cases for selling at the event. She knew this was going to make a huge dent in the available balance on the credit card, but she knew a lot of it would be recouped the day of the auction by selling wine by the glass which people could drink as they walked around and perused the auction items.

Jannelle was happy that the Raspberry Crisp wine was still available. Sal told her once the stock was gone it would be unavailable until the following year when it was made again at the local vineyard. She ordered four cases for the store and another case for her own personal wine cellar.

Sal told her Devon would make her delivery the following Friday as Thursday was Thanksgiving, and the Wine Depot would be closed. He gave her a hug and she left, feeling warm all over from all the wine she had tasted.

Jannelle pulled into the parking lot at the Denniston Rescue. There were very few cars, which made her wonder what was going on and why the place was so quiet. Then she remembered it was Monday, which was surgery day, so there were very few appointments scheduled for the day.

She grabbed a pile of flyers and headed inside. Through the glass door, Jannelle could see Cindy sitting behind the front desk with a frown on her face and her eyes closed. She only opened them when she heard the little bell sound on the door when Jannelle opened it. A loud argument could be heard coming from the vet's private office.

"What's going on?" Jannelle asked, walking up to the desk.

"Brandon Boles, Mary's fiancé, is in there. I assume they are fighting about her moving to Boston with him again," Cindy whispered. "He hates it here. She loves the Cape, and her job and doesn't want to move."

"That's too bad. If she leaves, though, we won't have a vet again. Last time, it took us forever to find another vet willing to take on the rescue and the vet hospital together."

"I know. Mary was an angel on earth when she showed up here that day to apply for the position. But that was before she got engaged and I think Brandon just assumed once they did, she would move like he wanted."

"Do you understand me?" Brandon's voice asked. "Do you know what you are giving up?"

"I understand perfectly. This engagement is over. Get your stuff out of my house and leave immediately," they heard Mary answer.

"I'm done with you," he screamed.

The argument got louder right before the door slammed open and Brandon flew out of the office in a rage, still screaming. He rushed past the two woman and left, leaving the front door wide open. Mary came out of her office, and it looked like she had been crying.

"Are you okay, Mary?" Cindy asked, rushing to her side.

"I am. It's over. You probably heard; I broke off my engagement with Brandon. I don't want to live in Boston, and I don't want to leave my job here, so I had no choice but to do what I did," she replied, taking a deep breath. "He gave me an ultimatum, so I set his ring on my desk and requested he leave."

"I'm so sorry," Jannelle said.

"Don't be. Things have been falling apart for a while now, but I never had the courage to do what I did before today. It can only get better from here on out," she replied. "I love my patients and any man who doesn't like animals is not the man for me."

"I know there are several men who live in the area, who love animals, and will be happy to know you are single again," Cindy said, trying to lighten the conversation.

"I can think of a couple myself," Jannelle added, smiling.

"Right now, the last thing I want is to start a new relationship. Brandon has to move his stuff out of my house, and I really and truly need to become *single* before I can even think of dating again. Now, Jannelle, did you need to see me about something?"

"Check this out," she replied, holding up one of the flyers for Mary to see.

"The Beautiful Yard donated a deck?" Mary asked in amazement. "I don't know what to say."

"I know, right? This is going to bring in lots of money for the rescue through the raffle sales. We've never had a donation like this before, not since we've been running the auction."

"I will have to thank Peter personally next time he brings in his dog, Pepper. If this works out as well as I think it will, we may be able to get that second-hand x-ray machine we've been needing," Mary stated. "It would be wonderful not have to send the animals four towns away to have x-rays done. We could treat them right here without any delay."

"I didn't know you were looking at x-ray machines," Jannelle said.

"I really wasn't. One of the smaller clinics in Yarmouth has been bought out by a larger company and one of the nurses there called me and informed me they would be selling all the equipment in the office. She wanted to know if I was interested in the machine as we had talked before, and I mentioned how great it would be to have one."

"Are they offering it at a decent price?" Cindy asked.

"They are. It's a portable machine but it would be just great for this office. I just don't have the cash on hand to buy it. But this raffle might afford me the money to do it," Mary replied. "Without blowing the yearly budget."

"When do you have to let them know by?" Jannelle asked.

"They have given me until December tenth. They said if I can come up with four thousand, they will hold it for me until January fifth to come up with the rest of the balance. That's when the clinic is closing and everything has to be removed from the building."

"So, how much do you need to hold it?"

"I have three thousand in the medical emergency fund. I would need another thousand to hold it. I applied for some grant money for a smaller one, but this one is better than the one I was originally looking at. And it's used, so it's not as expensive. Carrie told me the new company doesn't want to deal with the dispersing of the equipment and will be glad that someone is interested in it," Mary said.

"Call your friend and tell them you'll take it. I'm sure after this weekend we will have enough up front from the raffle to give you the money you need for the total down-payment. We can collect the money from the businesses in town on Sunday afternoon, after the long weekend of holiday shopping, and count it at our meeting Sunday night. We can get it to you on Monday morning," Jannelle said. "And I'm sure if we fall short people will pitch in until we have the amount you need."

"Really? This would be one of the best things this rescue could have," Mary replied. "I could treat the animals so much quicker if this machine was on site."

"Either Anita or I will bring you the money," Jannelle stated. "Cindy, please put the flyers up so people start to see the donation of the deck as the grand prize. I'm going to run. I have to stop by the Paint and Sip and make sure everything's okay."

"Thank you, Jannelle," Mary said, giving her a hug. "I'm going to go make that call right now."

"Don't thank me. It's a town effort," Jannelle replied, smiling and heading for the door.

"Hello? Anyone here?" Jannelle yelled as she entered the Paint and Sip.

"I'll be right with you," Anita answered from the office.

She stopped at the counter to take out the store credit card to return it to the safe in the office. Anita came rushing out of the office and stopped short when she saw who it was in the store.

"Oh, it's only you," she said. "I thought it was a real customer."

"Did the shipment come in today?"

"It just arrived about an hour ago. I haven't unpacked it yet."

"Nothing on backorder?" Jannelle asked.

"No, it's all there."

"Great! We need the pinecones for Saturday. We have twenty-three people scheduled for the class. I guess everyone wants a pinecone centerpiece for their Christmas table."

"This time I made sure we had plenty of spools of wire to attach the cones onto the frame. Last year we ran out and this year we won't. Plus, I ordered a variety of fake berries, sugared fruits and other brightly colored doodads they can decorate their pieces with," Anita added.

"It's your turn to pick a painting for next week's class. Have you gone down cellar to pick one out yet?"

"I did. I picked a pair of cardinals sitting in the birch trees in the snow. It's so pretty and it's perfect for heading into the winter season," Anita stated.

"I love that painting. I did that when my mother died. She always said she would come back as a cardinal and let me know she was okay after she passed. Those two cardinals were in my yard the day after her funeral, and I snapped their picture on my phone so I could paint it later."

"I didn't know that. I guess you really don't know everything about your best friend like you think you do," Anita replied.

"I know this is my day off, but we have a really large wine order coming in on Friday and I want to go downstairs and rotate the stock while you are here to watch the upstairs," Jannelle said,

"I'm assuming the credit card took a hit again?"

"It did. But we should be able to recoup most of it except for the one case I got for prizes and the three bottles that will accompany Picasso's paintings. If we sell a glass of wine for four dollars apiece during the auction, we will have no problem turning a profit."

"Awesome! I'm working on the end of month entries, so I'll be in the office."

"Can you put this back in the safe for me, please?" Jannelle asked, handing her the credit card.

Jannelle had just moved the first box when a loud crash and even louder scream came from above her. She ran up the stairs as fast as she could.

CHAPTER THREE

Anita was standing in the middle of the retail space, trembling. She was pointing to a brick laying on the floor in front of the smashed window in the door. There was a note tied to the brick with a piece of twine. Jannelle pulled out her cell phone and called Chief Stanton.

"Don't touch anything," Jannelle advised.

A crowd was beginning to gather outside.

"I'm going to see if anyone saw anything," Jannelle said.

"Don't you think we should wait for the chief to get here?"

"You know what they say. Sometimes the culprit hangs around to see what happens."

"The person is probably long gone by now. Why would someone do this? Do you think it's a kid's prank?"

"Not with a note attached to it. I wish the chief would get here so we can see what the note says," Jannelle replied.

"This used to be such a quiet little town," Anita said, sighing. "Wait until my husband hears about this. He'll be furious the rock was thrown with me standing right next to the door. It could have hit me."

"Sills! Camp! Set a perimeter around the door area," the chief ordered from outside. "Start to question the people in the area and see if they saw anything."

Jannelle led Anita to a chair. Gerald entered, looking around as he walked toward the women. He stopped at the brick and pulled out some plastic gloves before he picked it up.

"Nobody touched this, right?" he asked.

"We left it where it landed," Anita stated.

"Are you two women okay?"

"I was down in the cellar, but Anita was standing right near the door when it happened," Jannelle replied. "She's lucky she didn't get hit from the flying glass."

"Let's see what this note says," he said, untying the twine and opening the folded paper.

"Well, don't keep us in suspense. What does it say?" Jannelle asked.

"It says, stop meddling."

"What did you do now, Jannelle?' the chief asked. "Who did you make mad this time?"

"No one. And how do you know they're not talking about Anita?"

"Seriously? When has Anita ever made anyone mad?" Gerald replied.

"I guess, but I swear I haven't gotten involved in anyone else's business. I have no idea what the note means."

"Well, someone is pretty upset with one of you, or both of you, I don't know. Have you become involved in anything new lately or got any new students in your classes?"

"We always have new students," Anita stated.

"The only thing we have going on right now is the Jingle Bell Auction, but that event has been going on for five years now so that's nothing new."

"It's the second year it has been held here at the Paint and Sip and we didn't have any problems last year," Anita added.

"Anita!" Sid yelled through the broken window of the door. "Are you okay?"

"I'm fine. Come on in, just be careful where you walk," she replied to her husband.

"What happened? Who did this?" he asked, taking his wife's hand.

"We don't know," Jannelle answered.

"Have you got something in the cellar we can close off the broken window with?" Gerald asked.

"I think there's some plywood down there, or some boards," Jannelle stated.

"I'll go check," Sid said.

"I'll sweep up the broken glass," Anita said, heading to the backroom to get a broom.

"I don't know how much more we can do here, unless someone outside saw something," Gerald announced. "I hope it was just some kids playing a prank."

"Some prank," Jannelle said in disgust. "Excuse me while I call the hardware store and see if they can come replace the window tomorrow."

"I'm going outside to see if my deputies found out anything," Gerald said. "Now would be a great time to reconsider adding a camera system to your existing alarm system, both inside and out. I'll be in touch."

"I found a piece of plywood that will fit on the inside of the door. Do you have a hammer and some nails?" Sid asked, setting the wood next to the door while Anita finished sweeping.

Anita grabbed the hammer and some different sized nails from the back room and gave them to her husband. She finished sweeping and helped hold the board in place while Sid attached it to the door. Jannelle came out of the office, frowning.

"What's the matter?" Anita asked.

"Billy, the guy that does all the glass work for the hardware store went off Cape to visit his family for Thanksgiving. He won't be back until Friday."

"This board should stay in place until then. I can put a few extra nails in it if you'd like me to," Sid said.

"Please do. I don't want anyone getting into the store while we are closed for the holiday," Jannelle answered. "Billy will be here Friday morning to measure the window dimensions, and it should be replaced by late morning, so I was told."

"I just hope they don't decide to break the rest of our windows. Those big display windows would be expensive to replace," Anita stated, sighing.

"That's what you have insurance for," Sid replied. "But let's hope it doesn't happen."

"Why don't we close a little early today? Go home and have a glass of wine and relax with your husband. You're off tomorrow and will have time to recoup from what happened here," Jannelle suggested. "I'll be here tomorrow. I'm going to decorate the front window for Christmas and put Picasso's three paintings on display in amongst the decorations."

"I want to help," Anita said. "I love to decorate for the holidays."

"Don't worry. I'll leave the rest of the store for you to do."

"Promise?"

"I do. I'll do the two front windows and everything else will be up to you," Jannelle stated.

"I have some wonderful ideas for the store to get it ready for the auction," Anita said. "Maybe we can work on them together on Friday."

"Sounds good. Now go and have a glass of wine for me. Before I forget, do you still want Wednesday off for baking and preparing for Thanksgiving?"

"If that's okay."

"It's fine. I guess I'll see you on Friday morning. Have a great holiday with your family," Jannelle said, hugging her best friend. "Save me a piece of your peach pie."

"I will," Anita promised, walking out the door.

Shortly after her friend left, Jannelle closed the store and went home. She returned to the store the next day, Picasso's paintings in hand and started to decorate the larger of the two front windows. She set a round table in the corner of the space and placed a quilted tree skirt over it. A four-foot, fake Christmas tree was placed in the center of the table.

The tree was decorated with brightly colored twinkling lights, silver garland and a variety of hand-blown glass ornaments. Fluffy silver garland outlined the entire window and the wall space behind the tree. Jannelle carefully unwounds sheets of buffalo snow that had been used the previous year and covered the floor of the display space. She set up three easels and placed Picasso's paintings on them in a semi-circle facing the street.

In the lower corner of the window, she taped one of the auction's flyers up so people could see when the auction was and who it would benefit. The locals knew but any tourists still in the area in the off season might not. She stepped outside to look at her work.

The window was pretty, but it was missing something. She knew exactly what it was and returned inside to dig through the boxes of decorations she had brought up from the cellar. At the bottom of the box, was the can Jannelle was looking for.

"Spray snow," she said, holding up the can. "It's just what the window needs to be more festive."

She carefully stepped inside the display case and sprayed the front window leaving a large circle unsprayed in the center of the window. Going back outside, she clasped her hands together and sighed. It was perfect. The snow created a frame that showcased the tree and the paintings. It was like looking into a snow globe.

"One down and one to go," she said to herself.

In the second window, Jannelle built an artist's wonderland, showcasing the supplies and items offered for sale in the shop. She displayed several paintings the classes used to copy during paint and sip and several of the art pieces they created during Saturday art project classes. Twinkling lights framed the window and were weaved in and out of the products on the display. She finished the second window by spraying the snow in the same manner as she did in the first window.

She sat down to eat her lunch behind the register when she spotted a car slow down out front as it passed the store. Afraid they were going to receive another brick through the window, she ran for the front door and flung it open. Knowing he had been spotted, the car sped off. He left so fast that Jannelle couldn't even get a look at the license plate.

Jannelle placed a call to Gerald to tell him about the suspicious car and gave him a description of it.

Unfortunately, it was a common make of car so it wouldn't stick out if seen in town. She explained that he drove off so quickly she couldn't see the driver or get the plate. The chief asked again about cameras being installed at the store and Jannelle said she would look into it after Thanksgiving.

The rest of the day passed uneventfully as did the next day until Jannelle closed at noon for the holiday. She stopped at the grocery store on the way home to pick up her Thanksgiving order. It would save them time on Thanksgiving morning if they had one less delivery to make.

Her roommates met her at the door. Petunia stuck her head in the grocery bags that Jannelle had set down on the floor.

"That is not for you," she said, shooing the dog away. "Although, I'm sure you'll get some of it tomorrow."

The groceries were put away and Jannelle took Petunia for a nice long walk before it got dark outside. The puppy was pooped when they got back to the house and curled up in her bed for a nap. Picasso got his wet food and Jannelle sat down to watch the evening news. She ate a quick salad, and the family went to bed.

Thanksgiving morning greeted Jannelle with an early season snowstorm. She was glad she didn't have to go anywhere and could build a nice cozy fire, eat her turkey meal, and read for the majority of the day. Petunia loved the warmth of the fire and dragged her doggie bed in front of the hearth, turned a few circles and laid down, sighed deeply, and fell asleep.

The snow stopped early afternoon with an accumulation of around four inches on the ground. Jannelle heard the plows go by out on the main road. She watched some television, did some more reading and then made herself an open-faced turkey sandwich, slathering it with warmed-up gravy.

She took Petunia out before it got dark for her final outing before bed. Petunia didn't like the snow at all. It rubbed against her belly and her little legs were lost underneath the white stuff as she walked. Once inside, the dog finished her supper quickly and was back in front of the fire warming up as her owner watched the six o'clock news.

Picasso had an extra lazy holiday, not moving from the bay window. He had batted at the snowflakes as they passed the panes earlier in the day and when bored with that, slept the rest of the day.

"Is this what you do while I'm gone all day?" she asked the cat, who finally jumped down out of the window in search of some supper. "It's a wonder you're not ten pounds heavier than you are."

Jannelle finished the book she was reading and figured it was time for bed as she had to be at the shop early in the morning for the wine delivery. She made sure the screen was tight against the stones of the fireplace so no embers could escape until the fire burned out completely. Tucking Petunia under one arm and calling for the cat, she climbed the stairs to get ready for bed.

Along with the early snow, the colder temperatures had also arrived. Jannelle went in search of some gloves she had packed away the previous winter. The snow needed to be cleared off the car and Petunia needed to go on her morning walk and she wasn't going to do either bare-handed.

Knowing she wouldn't be home until later that evening, she decided to take Petunia with her as the dog could be contained in the office behind a gate during the wine delivery. Picasso would jump the gate and be out the door in a flash. The last time he got out, he ran into the woods behind the shop, and it took Jannelle over an hour to find him.

"I'll take you to the shop tomorrow," she promised the cat. "I'm sure everyone in the class would like to visit with you, and I know you'll be right in the middle of everything, batting around the pinecones."

The roads were clear, and Jannelle was at the shop earlier than she planned. She let Petunia run around in the shop until she unlocked the front door to open to customers and then the dog was secured in the back room behind a gate. Anita arrived shortly after nine. Petunia greeted her at the back door, her tail wagging like crazy, showing her happiness to see her friend.

"Hello, beautiful. I had a feeling you'd be here today. Look what I brought you," Anita said, taking out a peanut butter cookie and handing it to the dog.

Petunia loved the homemade cookies that Anita baked and brought her. She trotted off to the office where her bed was with her prize.

"She loves those cookies," Jannelle said, smiling. "Maybe you should bake some and we could sell them here in the shop. A lot of our customers have dogs at home."

"We could try that," Anita replied. "It's not food for humans so we wouldn't need a permit to sell them."

"The wine order should be here shortly. I wonder which lady friend will be helping Devon on his route today," Jannelle said.

"I don't know, but I did hear a little bit of gossip at the grocery store this morning that might interest you and maybe even the chief."

"About what?"

"It seems that after the special meeting the other night that you attended and spoke up at, Cynthia Parsons was not given the job as town administrator."

"And what does that have to do with me?"

"The board took your objections into consideration when they made their decision to offer the job to someone else," Anita replied, taking her coat off.

"I merely pointed out the fact that she was fired from an off-Cape position for suspicion of taking bribes. It was public knowledge and in all the newspapers."

"You also said you didn't know if she could be trusted in the position she was applying for. It made a big impact on the decision. And Cynthia is none too happy with you and told several people she would get even with you for costing her the job."

"Can I help it if I say what needs to be said when everyone else is sitting around and just thinking it?"

"No, you always tell it like it is, even if it gets you in trouble sometimes. At least people know where they stand with you and that you won't pull punches."

"Do you think it was her who threw the brick through the window?" Janelle asked her friend.

"I don't know, but it would probably be worth mentioning it to the chief so he can check it out," Anita replied.

"I'll call him right after the wine delivery. Devon's truck just pulled up to the loading dock."

Thirty-two cases of wine were taken downstairs. Devon left and Jannelle sorted the cases, putting the store wine in one pile, the auction wine in another pile, and the prize wine in another. The three cases she ordered for her own stock at home, were carried back upstairs and left near the back door.

"Don't forget to call the chief and let him know about Cynthia and her threat," Anita said, working to untangle a string of Christmas lights.

"I'm doing it right now," Janelle replied, pulling out her phone.

"We don't have class until tomorrow night so I'm leaving the strings of light spread out on the floor until I put them up tomorrow," Anita said when Jannelle returned from making her call. "What did the chief say?"

"He said he would look into it. I'm going to take Petunia out back to let her go and I'll be right back to help you with the rest of the lights."

As Jannelle walked the perimeter of the parking lot with the dog, a car pulled up next to her. The tinted window rolled down and Cynthia was sitting in the driver's seat.

"Hello, Jannelle," she said.

"What can I do for you, Cynthia?"

"I just wanted to thank you in person for causing me to lose the admin job."

"Is that why you threw the brick through the store window?" Jannelle asked, watching her face for a reaction.

"I did no such thing."

"You were the only person to have a reason to do it."

"*You* do realize the charges against me were never proven. I never did anything outside the limit of the law," Cynthia stated. "That's not why I came to see you."

"And why would that be?" Jannelle asked as Petunia pulled on the leash, wanting to move on.

"I actually came to thank you. Because I didn't get the admin job, I was offered a different job, a better paying one in Orleans. If I had signed the contract for the town, I wouldn't have been free to accept the secretary position with the higher salary I will be getting now."

"I'm glad things worked out for you," Jannelle said.

"And besides, why would I throw a brick through the window when I signed up to attend the painting classes after the holidays? I know people look down on me for what they think I did, according to the newspapers, but I was hoping to get a fresh start here in town and put my past behind me."

"As long as you promise me it wasn't you who threw the brick through the window, you will be welcome here for class," Jannelle replied. "Now, I have to go. Petunia is not one to sit still for very long."

"I will see you at the auction," Cynthia yelled as she drove away.

"Who was that in the car?" Anita asked as Jannelle entered the shop from her dog walking.

"That was Cynthia. She came to thank me for screwing up her chance of getting the town job."

"Excuse me? She thanked you?"

Jannelle repeated the conversation she had just had outside to Anita.

"I have to admit, she did sign up for all four of the January paint and sip classes. Several weeks ago, as a matter of fact. I forgot she came in since we've had such a rash of new people signing up for something to do during the winter."

"I guess I'll call the chief back and tell him to forget about looking into Cynthia," Jannelle said. "So, it looks like we are back to square one as to who threw the brick."

"It's almost five. I promised Sid I would meet him at the café for our Friday night special dinner. Do you mind closing up?" Anita asked. "I'll finish up the decorations in the morning before tomorrow night's class."

"Sure, go ahead. Petunia and I will close up. I'll see you in the A.M."

Petunia trotted out of the office with a stuffed candy corn in her mouth looking for someone to play with her. She set it at Jannelle's feet and waited for her to throw it.

"I'll throw it once but then we have to get ready to go home," she said, picking up the toy and throwing it into the backroom. "It's two past five so I guess I can lock the door for the day."

Jannelle made her way to the front of the store and locked the door. She stopped at the window to straighten out one of Picasso's paintings that had gone a little cock-eyed on its easel.

A car was parked in front of the store going the wrong way on the street. The man in the car quickly pulled down his ballcap when he saw he had been spotted and sped off into the night.

CHAPTER FOUR

Jannelle pulled out her phone and called the station. She told them about the car and how suspiciously the man acted when he was seen. It happened too quickly to get a plate number or get a clear view of the driver. All she could tell them was it was a newer model, dark-colored sedan. They promised to keep an eye out and watch the store overnight.

Once home, the animals were fed, and Jannelle started her own supper. She ate her microwave mac and cheese while watching the weather. More snow was predicted for the following day.

"Boy, the snow is hitting us early this year. I suppose after last year of very little snow, we can't complain this year," she said to Picasso who had hopped up on the foot of the recliner and was cleaning himself after finishing his supper. "I'm glad I got the new tires put on when I did."

Petunia was patiently waiting at the side of the recliner for a noodle covered with cheese. Jannelle gave her one and told her to go lay down, which she did.

"I guess you'll have to come to the shop with me tomorrow, Petunia. If it is snowing, I won't have the time to come back to the house and let you out before the class begins. Picasso, I'm sure you'll be fine here by yourself," she said, scratching the cat's ears.

It was flurrying as Jannelle left the house the next morning. Petunia was locked into her doggie seat in the back seat of the car and was happily looking out the window as they headed to town. Anita was already at the store finishing up the Christmas decorating before it opened for business.

"We've had two cancellations for tonight. Mrs. Valentine and Mrs. Collins don't want to leave their houses," Anita said as Jannelle took off her coat.

"That's understandable. They're both in their eighties and probably don't want to drive in the snow. The store looks beautiful."

Anita had strung up twinkling lights around the two rooms and around the door to the back room. Sparkly snowflakes hung from the ceiling and danced each time the door was opened. Various sized snowmen were placed around the shop along with beautifully wrapped presents. A table-top tree had been decorated and set on one end of the wine table. This is where the Secret Santa gifts would be placed as they were brought in for the store Christmas Party.

"Look in the back room," Anita said.

A large sleigh, filled with cellophane bags, tied up with red and green ribbons, was sitting on the table. Petunia was sitting underneath it, whining.

"You made your dog cookies," Jannelle said. "Petunia can smell them and is waiting for one."

"I left some in a small jar on the desk in the office for Petunia," Anita replied. "I wasn't sure where you wanted to put them or how much to charge for them."

"Let's put them on the counter next to the register. And I want you to set a price because I want you to take the money for your own Christmas shopping. It can be your little side business," Jannelle said, opening the jar and giving Petunia a cookie.

"Are you sure? I made them to be sold in the shop," Anita protested.

"I'm sure. There is nothing in the rules that says we can't do a little something for ourselves once in a while," Jannelle replied, giving Petunia a cookie.

"Like taking home a bottle of wine we really like once in a while," Anita said, chuckling.

"Exactly. The snow is really starting to come down now. I bet we have a few more cancellations before the day are over," Jannelle said, looking out the front door window. "It's so nice to have the window back in the door."

"It is supposed to be nice and sunny tomorrow. We won't be open, but the local shops will hopefully have some good holiday shoppers around who will buy some of the raffle tickets."

"I hope we have enough money on the presales to bring to Mary at the rescue so she can make the down-payment on the x-ray machine on Monday," Jannelle added.

"Everyone I've talked to say the sales are doing awesome since the deck was added for the grand prize. I don't know if we'll ever be able to top this year after that donation," Anita replied. "Sid and I are going to do a bit of Christmas shopping tomorrow. He's going to walk around Main Street with me while I collect the presale money."

"That's good. I feel safer with you having Sid with you."

"I don't think anyone would know any different as we take our weekly stroll around town every Sunday and then go to the diner for brunch," Anita stated. "Oh, no, there's the phone. I bet it's another cancellation. I'll get it."

Jannelle unlocked the front door. The snow was coming down so heavily she couldn't see the shops across the street. The street was pretty much empty for a Saturday, and really empty for a Saturday shopping day after Thanksgiving.

"That was Millie. The sheriff has the evening shift, and she doesn't want to drive here by herself so she cancelled for tonight."

"Maybe we should just cancel the class and have the pinecone class next Saturday," Jannelle suggested. "What do you think? Should we call everyone on the list that signed up?"

"It might be for the best. Even if the snow lets up, the roads will have to be plowed and everyone will have to dig out of their own driveways. I think it will be safer for everyone to stay home," Anita replied. "I'll go into the office and make the calls."

An hour later, the calls had all been made and the women stood looking out the front window trying to decide whether they should stay open or not. The walk at the front of the store needed to be shoveled. Jannelle threw on her coat and ran out to push the snow away from the entrance.

Noon rolled around and they hadn't had even one customer. The street was pretty much void of cars except for the occasional passing plow. Anita set to work picking up all the items that had been set out for making the pinecone centerpieces. The Thursday class would be a paint and sip, so the easels needed to be set on the tables along with the disposable palettes.

"It looks like the other shops on Main Street are closing up because of the weather. What do you want to do?" she asked Anita.

"I seriously don't think anyone will be out shopping right now. I say we follow suit and go home. We'll meet back here tomorrow night for the meeting of the Jingle Bell Auction committee."

"I'll lock up if you want to head out," Jannelle said.

"Be careful going home," Anita said as she headed out the back door.

"I think the snow is up to your belly," Jannelle said to the dog. "Maybe I'll pick you up and carry you to the car, so you don't get your little seat all wet."

She picked up the dog, set the alarm at the back door and headed for her car. As she was securing Petunia in her seat, she looked through the window and saw the same car that had passed in front of her shop parked at the other end of the parking lot. She quickly closed the door to keep the dog safe and grabbed her phone. The man sitting in the car saw he had been noticed and that Jannelle was on her phone. He took off out of the far exit and disappeared in the swirling snow.

"Who is that guy?" she said, thinking out loud as the dispatcher answered her call.

"Excuse me?"

Jannelle explained why she had placed the call and requested the sheriff be informed about what was called in to the station. The police on duty needed to know the car was still in the area as they were on the lookout for it. She finished her call and took out her snowbrush to clear her windows to drive home.

Petunia watched as her owner walked around the car. Jannelle played peek-a-boo with the dog when she cleaned off the window next to the dog seat. She took a final look around for the mysterious car and satisfied it was nowhere near, she started the car and let it warm up a bit before heading off.

"You were such a good girl waiting for me to finish," she said, handing Petunia a cookie that she had brought out with her from inside.

All the way home, she kept glancing out her rear-view mirror making sure no headlights were following behind her. It was slow going even though the roads had already been plowed once. The snow accumulated faster than the plows could get to all the streets.

"This was supposed to be a light snow, not a blizzard," she said to the dog as they neared her driveway. "But we made it home."

She turned into the driveway and a dark sedan went speeding by the back end of her car.

"Great! He followed me home. Let's get you to go the bathroom fast and get in the house and lock up," Jannelle said, parking as close as she could to the back porch.

The side of the house, facing away from the wind, had very little snow on the ground and Petunia headed right to that spot to do her business. Picasso met them at the door. Jannelle locked the deadbolt and peered out the door window looking for any headlights in the area but saw nothing.

She picked up Picasso and gave him some loving. He purred loudly and rubbed his face against her chin.

"Did you miss me?" she asked him. "You've been here by yourself quite a bit lately."

She set the cat down and he strolled off to see where Petunia had gone to. The light was flashing on her answering machine, so she walked over to check it. The first four messages were for new donations for the auction. She quickly scribbled the names and the items they would be donating on a notepad she kept next to the phone. The new prizes would be added to the inventory list, and she would announce them at the meeting the following night.

It was the last message that drew her attention.

"I warned you to mind your own business, but you didn't listen, Now, you will pay the consequences. I hope your meddling will be worth it to you."

She called the station right away and asked to speak to Chief Stanton as she knew he was on duty from three to eleven. Jannelle told him about the threat on her message machine and how the car had followed her home. He asked that she not erase the message as he would be over first thing in the morning to listen to it. He ended the call by telling her to be careful and to make sure every door and window at her house was locked.

"Well, it looks like you two will be coming with me wherever I go until they catch this guy," she said. "I would be devastated if anything happened to you, and I don't like the tone of his words. Better safe than sorry."

The animals followed her into the kitchen. Jannelle opened the fridge to see what she could whip up for an early supper. She had an electric stove and if the power went out she wouldn't be able to cook.

"Scrambled eggs and bacon sound good," she said, pulling the needed items out and placing them on the counter next to the stove. "And I'm sure you two wouldn't refuse a few pieces of bacon."

She fed her roommates their supper and fixed her own. A short time later, she was sitting in her recliner with the cat on the foot section and Petunia sitting next to the chair, looking up at her. They waited patiently while Jannelle ate and were each rewarded with two pieces of bacon.

The dirty dishes were brought to the kitchen. Jannelle poured herself a big glass of peach wine and settled in with a book she had half finished. Her mind kept wandering to the message on her answering machine. She had heard that voice before, but where? Not being able to concentrate on the book, she set it aside and turned on her TV.

Saturday nights weren't a very good night on television. She settled on a repeat of one of her favorite forensic shows and pulled an over-sized sherpa blanket over her. The cat settled in at her feet and Petunia tucked herself in next to her owner's leg. Her eyes closed here and there as she relaxed. Both animals were asleep and snoring.

Jannelle opened her eyes and let out a scream. Behind her, a man's face looking in the bay window reflected in the screen of the TV set. He ran for it once he knew she saw him. She jumped out of the chair, dumping Picasso on the floor and burying Petunia in the blanket. Running to get her bat, she headed to the kitchen to see if she could see anything out the door window that faced the street in front of her house.

As she peered through the falling snow, a face, covered completely in a black ski mask, popped up from the bottom of the door. The person slammed their hands on the window which made Jannelle almost jump out of her skin with fear. She raised her bat, and the figure ran off. Jannelle watched the person run down the driveway and up the street until she lost him as he went out of reach of the streetlight beam.

Petunia was running around in the kitchen, barking. She picked up the dog and talked to her quietly to calm her down. Jannelle gave her a new pig's ear and put Petunia in her bed in the living room. She searched for Picasso next. He had run upstairs in all the commotion and stayed at the top of the stairs looking at her, not wanting to come back down.

Jannelle dialed the chief again. She told him what had happened, and he promised to send someone out there to talk to her and maybe find some footprints of the intruder. She poured herself some more wine and waited for the police. Twenty minutes later, Deputy Camp arrived. He walked around in the yard with a flashlight checking for footprints.

Next, he came into the house to take Jannelle's statement. He wrote down the description of the person at the door and used his cell phone to make a recording of the phone call made earlier to take back to the chief. He promised Jannelle they would pass by her house several times during the night and that they were still looking for the dark sedan. He left after making sure she locked the door behind him.

Deciding they had enough excitement for one night, she scooped up her animals and went upstairs. Jannelle didn't know if it was all the commotion, or maybe the wine, but she slept soundly through the night.

The sun was shining the next morning. Altogether, the snow had amounted to about six to eight inches.

She had her morning coffee, took the dog out and then secured them in the house so she could shovel her driveway and clean off her car before she had to go out for the meeting later on at the store.

"I have got to get someone to plow the driveway," she said, looking around as she shoveled. "It seems to get longer and longer with each passing year."

Luckily, it was a light, fluffy snow which was easy to push aside rather than pick up by the shovel full. Picasso watched out the bay window. Jannelle threw several snowballs at the cat who batted at the snow as it slipped down the windowpane. She finally reached the end of the driveway where the plows had made quite the pile overnight. Shoveling that twenty-foot distance across took her longer than doing the whole rest of the driveway and walks combined.

"That was a lot of work," she said to the cat as she took her boots off in the mudroom. "I need some lunch."

The rest of the day was spent snuggled in the chair with her two furry roommates reading the book she needed to return to the library the next day. An hour before she had to leave for her meeting, she gathered all her paperwork together she needed to present at the meeting and gave Picasso and Petunia their supper.

Jannelle and the animals arrived at the Paint and Sip shortly before the meeting was to begin. She put up the gate to keep Petunia in the back room and the office. Picasso could jump the gate, but he had never tried to escape out the front door as people came in and went out.

Six o'clock arrived and Anita hadn't arrived yet, which was strange as she usually beat Jannelle there for the meetings. Cars started to park out front, and the committee members came in for the meeting. Still, no Anita.

"Millie, have you talked to Anita today?" Jannelle asked.

"I ran into her in town when her and Sid were picking up the donation money from the various businesses," she replied. "But other than that, no."

"I'm getting worried. She's not here yet and she always beats me here," Jannelle stated. "I'm going to call Sid. Excuse me."

She placed her call and came back to the group with a frown on her face.

"What's the matter?" Millie asked.

"I just talked to Sid, and he said Anita left half an hour ago. She should have been here by now. I've called her cell phone, and she doesn't answer it."

"Have you checked the back parking lot where she usually parks?" Sally asked, joining the group. "Maybe she fell on ice or slick snow."

"I'll do that right now," Jannelle said, stepping over the gate.

She picked up Petunia so she wouldn't run out the door and peered out. Anita's car was parked in her usual parking space, but she wasn't in it. Jannelle locked Petunia in the office and called to Millie to grab her coat and join her. They walked around the car and saw Anita's cell phone on the front seat, along with her purse whose contents had been emptied and scattered about.

"Millie, call your husband. I think something has happened to Anita," Jannelle requested.

As Millie placed the call, Jannelle opened the front door of the car and looked around without touching anything. The keys were still in the ignition. She made note that the deposit bag for the auction fund was not among the things left behind. Stepping away from the car, she called Sid and told him he better get to the store.

Two cruisers came screaming into the parking lot with lights and sirens going full force. Sheriff Stanton followed in his own vehicle as he was home on his day off. Sid arrived and rushed to the car where everyone was standing.

"Where is my wife?" Sid asked. "What's going on?"

"We don't know. She made it here but after she arrived, she never made it inside," Jannelle answered. "Sid, did Anita have the money you collected today with her?"

"She did. We had collected almost four thousand dollars from the various businesses around town as we took our Sunday stroll. Why?'

"I don't see any money in her purse and the deposit bag we usually use for the auction money isn't in the car," Jannelle replied.

"Do you think this was a robbery?" the chief asked.

"It looks like it, but why take Anita if they only wanted the money?" Jannelle asked.

"Maybe she recognized who it was who was robbing her," Sheriff Stanton answered. "Sid, did you notice anyone following you around today as you went from business to business?"

"Not that I can recall," Sid replied.

"Chief, you might want to take a look at this," Deputy Camp said.

CHAPTER FIVE

Taped to the underside of Anita's purse was a piece of paper. It read CONSEQUENCES in big red letters.

"Camp, take that to the station and run it for prints," Stanton directed.

"What does that mean, consequences?" Sid asked, choking out the words.

"Unfortunately, Sid, it means Anita was taken on purpose. It wasn't just a robbery like we first thought," the chief replied.

"Is this tied to the brick that was thrown through the window?" Sid asked.

"I'm afraid so. This person means business and he's been one step ahead of us this whole time."

"I have been wracking my brain trying to figure out what we meddled in, and I keep coming up with nothing," Jannelle said. "I just don't understand."

"Think, Jannelle," Sid said. "Has anything changed at the store?"

"No, nothing. The only thing that is different is we are working on the Jingle Bell Auction, but we have done that for the last five years."

"Is the money still benefiting the Denniston Animal Rescue?" the chief asked.

"Yes, just like it has since the auction started," she replied. "Oh, dear."

"What? Did you think of something?" Sid asked.

"Not in regard to Anita, but in regard to the rescue."

"What?"

"We were supposed to give one thousand dollars to Mary at the rescue tomorrow morning so she could put a deposit on an x-ray machine for the rescue. Now, she may lose the machine because the money is gone. That's why you and Anita collected some of the money early because we were working under a deadline," Jannelle stated.

"Who else knew the money was being used for the x-ray machine?" the chief asked.

"Myself, Anita, the committee, and Mary and Cindy at the rescue."

"Are you sure no one else overheard you talking about it?" Sid asked.

"No, I'm not sure. There were a few people at the rescue, but I didn't notice anyone paying particular attention to our conversation."

"It doesn't make sense. Why would anyone in town steal the money meant for the rescue? It has been well supported and Mary is loved by all those who have pets that she treats. The x-ray machine would only make things better for the rescue," Sid stated. "And why take my Anita? Is it because she's involved in the auction?"

"I don't know," Jannelle mumbled.

"We need to tape off this whole area. Jannelle, do you want to move your car before we do?" the chief asked.

"Please, I need to get home later. May I go inside and call Mary to tell her what has happened? I guess the rescue will lose the x-ray machine now unless we can come up with the money that was stolen. I'm going inside to cancel the meeting. We don't need to have it now as Anita usually runs it," Jannelle said.

She went inside the store and explained the circumstances of what had happened to the rest of the women who were waiting in the front studio. They all agreed to do what they could to help find Anita and left. Jannelle sat at the table in the back room watching the police through the window do what they needed to do. The shop phone rang.

"Hello."

"I told you there'd be consequences."

"Who is this and what have you done with Anita?" Jannelle demanded, while knocking on the window to get the chief's attention.

"Cancel the auction or you will never see your friend alive again. Do you understand me?"

The chief came through the door and Jannelle handed him the phone.

"Who is this?"

The line went dead.

"What did they say?" he asked a shaken Jannelle.

"He said if I didn't cancel the auction, I would never see Anita alive again," she replied as she turned to see Sid standing in the door, the color draining from his face.

"Was it the same person who called your house and left the message there?"

"It was. I know I have heard the voice somewhere before, but I can't place it or where I have heard it," she replied.

"Do you think it's another local?" Sid asked.

"I just don't know," Jannelle replied, frowning.

"Do you think they have already hurt my wife?" Sid asked, sitting down in a chair close to him.

"I don't think so, Sid. It seems more important to them that they get what they want rather than hurting Anita. Stay positive. We will find her, and she'll be fine," the chief insisted. "We did find some footprints adjacent to Anita's car and made casts of them. We dusted the door handle and have taken everything else in the car to see if we can find any prints."

"Find her, Gerald. Please. I can't live without my wife," Sid pleaded.

"We'll find her. You need to go home in case someone calls you there," the chief advised him. "I will stay in touch."

They watched Sid walk out the door, slowly and dejected. In the silence, they could hear Petunia whining in the office.

"In all the hoopla, I forgot she was in there. She probably needs to go out," Jannelle said, opening the office door.

"Go straight home and make sure the house is locked up tight. These people aren't playing around. Taking Anita has stepped this up to a whole new level. I have something I have to take care of, but I will call if I learn anything," the chief said. "We have done all we can out back for now but will leave the parking lot taped off in case we can find something tomorrow in the daylight."

"Do you have your taser with you?"

"I do, but so did Anita and see how much good it did for her," Jannelle replied, snapping the leash on Petunia's harness.

"Just be careful," the chief said, going out the back door.

Jannelle secured the front door of the store, turned out the lights and set the alarm at the back door. Picasso's crate was set in the back seat. She let Petunia walk around a bit and do her thing before they got in the car to go home. She knew she would have to get up earlier than usual on a Monday to get her errands done before she came to open the store where Anita wouldn't be working.

Jannelle drove home in silence. She knew she had heard that voice before, but where? The animals had already had an early supper, so she set to work putting together a salad for her supper. Petunia was already in her bed in front of the fireplace and Picasso had curled up in the bay window.

"I definitely have to do some food shopping," she said, whacking the bottom of the Russian dressing bottle to get out the last little amount that she could.

She finished her salad, even though she wasn't really hungry. Jannelle ran person after person through her mind trying to match the voice to someone she knew. She dozed off while waiting for the weather to begin. Petunia woke her up around twelve-thirty, whining to go out.

"I don't like to take you out this late," she said. "We're going to stay right next to the porch and then it's right back inside."

Petunia finished and they were back in the house without incidence. Twenty minutes later, the family was in bed.

Jannelle was up at seven, making coffee and texting Sid to see if he had heard anything from Anita. The answer was no. He didn't sound very good, and he stated he had been up all night long waiting for the phone to ring. She hung up, promising to call him later.

"Come on, kiddos, no one stays home by themselves," she said, fighting to get Picasso in his crate. "Not until this whacko is caught."

Jannelle ran into the library and dropped her books in the return slot. She didn't stick around to get new ones as the animals were in the car and she had to get to the Paint and Sip to open for the day's business.

Petunia was secured behind the gate and Picasso had found his usual spot in the front window. She put the money in the register and went to check the phone for any new messages. There were none.

"Oh, Anita, where are you?" she said as she unlocked the front door for business.

The morning had been quiet except for the occasional person coming in to inquire whether there was any word on Anita yet. Jannelle ate her lunch, sitting at the register, next to the shop phone. The little bell on the door sounded. Jannelle looked up to see someone she never expected to be in the store.

"Hello, Jannelle," Karen Kramer said.

"Karen, what brings you into our little store," Jannelle asked, putting down her sandwich.

"I just wanted to be the good local and check to see if there was any word on Anita yet."

"No, there isn't and I'm worried sick."

"Have the police figured out anything yet?"

"Not yet, but they're working on it. They found footprints next to Anita's car."

"They found footprints?"

"Yes, but the chief hasn't got back to me about them yet."

"How is the auction going? I see Picasso's paintings in the front window," Karen asked, picking up a bag of baked dog cookies and tossing them back into the sleigh. "Anita was putting so much effort into making it a success this year."

"It's going to be a success. Nothing about that has changed because of Anita's disappearance. As a matter of fact, this will be our best year yet thanks to your ex-husband donating the deck as the grand prize."

"Don't remind me. He'll do anything to get on Mary Pimms' good side," Karen muttered under her breath.

"Do you have a problem with Mary? She is one of the best vets in the New England region," Jannelle asked.

"No, I just don't like animals much, any of them. She seems like such a goody-goody, and everyone thinks she's so sweet. I knew her in college, and she was a total wild child."

"People change, and she is sweet and a wonderful human being. And most of us in this town love our animals and she takes phenomenal care of them," Jannelle replied. "Sounds like it's more that you're jealous that Peter is paying attention to our town's vet."

"We're divorced and it was me who broke it off. Do you understand me? I broke it off, not Peter. I hated that stupid dog that he had. He paid more attention to it than me. Now he can spend all the time he wants to with that mutt."

"Whatever you say."

"Are you still going to have the auction with Anita gone? She *was* in charge of it again like last year, wasn't she?"

"I'm sure Anita will be back long before the auction and yes, she is in charge of it, and yes, the auction will take place as planned," Jannelle said,

"I guess that's a good thing for the rescue," Karen said, frowning and rolling her eyes.

"What do you want, Karen? Why did you really come in here?" Jannelle asked, growing impatient.

"I told you; I am checking on Anita," she replied. "I guess I got my answer, so I'll go now."

"Have a great day," Jannelle said sarcastically as Karen opened the door.

"And you wonder why people don't frequent your establishment," Karen replied, slamming the door as she left.

"What a jerk! I wonder what Peter ever saw in her," Jannelle said to Picasso who had come to see what his owner was eating. "And we all know it was Peter who filed for divorce, not her."

She sat down to finish her sandwich when the shop phone rang.

"Hello, Paint and Sip. How may I help you?"

"Obviously, you don't value your friend's life. Cancel the auction today or she is done for. DO you understand me?"

Before she could answer, the line went dead. Jannelle immediately called the chief to report the call. He wanted permission to get the shop's phone records to see if they could trace where the call was coming from.

She asked the chief what he thought as to whether or not she should cancel the auction. He told her to hold off until they got the phone records and not act hastily. She promised to hold off until he said so.

Jannelle called Mary next to inform her of the chance the auction might be cancelled. As upset as Mary was about the auction, she was more upset about Anita being abducted. When Jannelle asked her how she found out about what had happened, figuring maybe it was the high-lighted gossip around town, Mary told her the chief told her what had happened when he dropped off a check for one-thousand dollars so she could put the deposit on the x-ray machine.

Jannelle was happy that the chief would do that, but it didn't shock her he would take it upon himself to make sure the rescue got the machine. He had assured Mary they would recover the stolen money, and she could pay him back when they did. But this way, the x-ray machine was secure in its purchase. Mary had gone that very morning to put the deposit on it.

She was just about to ask Mary about Karen and if she really had gone to the same college as her, but at the last second she decided to keep Karen's visit a secret, except from the chief.

The business for the day picked up in the afternoon. Several people came in and signed up for Saturday's painting class after asking if it would still be held with Anita missing. Trying to sound upbeat, she assured them that she thought Anita would be back before then.

The art director for the elementary school came in to drop off a list of supplies she needed for the after-school program. Carrie had worked with both Jannelle and Anita at various school events, so she knew them both well, and she took over the position of art teacher for the school system when Jannelle retired.

"I saw Karen Kramer in here earlier when I walked past the store. What did that troublemaker want?" Carrie asked.

"She claims she was checking on Anita's disappearance." Jannelle replied.

"I highly doubt that. Karen doesn't look out for anyone but herself. That's one of the reasons Peter dumped her. She wouldn't get a job, and she blew through all his money, except for the inheritance he received from his dad. He wouldn't let her touch that," Carrie stated.

"How do you know all this?"

"Peter is my stepbrother. We are very close. His marriage to Karen was a nightmare and he transferred all the inheritance to me to protect her from getting her hands on it."

"Interesting. Now that the divorce is final, do you still have control of the money? If you don't mind me asking," Jannelle said.

"Yes, I do. She keeps coming up with new ways to drag him back to court to try to get her half of it even though the judge told her the money was Peter's before they were married, and she wasn't entitled to it. The judge continues to throw out every case she brings with the same answer."

"How is she living?" Jannelle asked.

"He got stuck paying her alimony. But it's in the divorce decree that if either of them remarries, it stops, and she'll get nothing from that point on. I pity the poor sucker she finds next to marry," Carrie replied.

That's why Karen doesn't want Peter to be interested in any other woman.

"So, can I pick the supplies up next Monday?" Carrie asked.

"I place my order tomorrow morning, and it gets delivered on Thursdays, but I will hold it for you until next Monday if that's when you want to pick it up," Jannelle replied.

"Thanks. I hope you hear something on Anita sooner than later. It bothers me that something like this could happen to such a wonderful woman and in our small town. I guess the world is changing and nowhere is safe now. If I hear anything, I'll let you know immediately."

"If you hear anything, please call the chief right away," Jannelle requested.

"I will. See you next week," Carrie said, heading for the door.

"Well, at least we know why Karen is upset because Peter likes Mary," Jannelle said to Petunia. "Do you need to go out?"

The dog turned a couple of circles and ran for the back door. Jannelle put a sign up in the front window, *dog walking, be back in ten minutes*. She locked the front door and took Petunia out the back door. When they returned, the store landline was ringing, and Jannelle ran to answer it.

"Hello."

"This is Deputy Camp. The chief wanted me to call you and let you know that the two sets of footprints found next to Anita's car were made by one female and one male."

"Really. So, we have a team working together. Will you have the chief call me at his earliest convenience. I have something to discuss with him," Jannelle asked, wanting to tell him about the two conversations that took place in the store.

"Anita, where are you?" Jannelle said, thinking out loud. "I think I'll stop and check on Sid on my way home. You two will be okay in the car for ten minutes or so."

People drifted in and out the rest of the afternoon while Jannelle stayed at the register so she would be near the phone. She never heard from Anita's captors again.

When she stopped to check on Sid, she found several other locals there doing the same thing. Some had brought him some casseroles and others were just there chatting with him. She stayed a few minutes and promised to call him if she found out anything about his wife.

Jannelle poured herself a glass of wine and sat at the kitchen table while her roommates ate their supper. She thought to herself she could say the auction had been cancelled and see if whoever was holding Anita would release her and after she was safe, reinstate the event. But it would be difficult to stop the auction now as people had spent money on tickets and donated so many items.

"What should I do?" she asked Picasso who was rubbing up against her leg. "I have to concentrate and figure out where I have heard that voice on the phone before."

The phone rang. Jannelle hesitated to answer it in case it was the kidnapper again. She didn't want to lie and say the auction had been cancelled because if he found out it hadn't been he could hurt Anita. She decided to let it go to the answering machine, but no message was left as the line went dead when the recording to leave a message started to recite itself.

Then her mind wandered to where they could be holding Anita. There were many places in town that were remote enough to hide someone. There were houses all over town, all closed up as they were owned by people who were only here during the summer months. If the person was desperate enough to kidnap someone, they would surely break into a vacant house to use it.

Jannelle made a quick ham and cheese sandwich with a big chunk of a deli pickle for supper. She refilled her wine and ate right at the table instead of sitting in front of the TV. She was in the process of taking the dog out for the last time of the night, when she saw two coyotes wandering around in the yard.

"Looks like we have to wait a bit," she said to Petunia.

Several minutes later the coyotes wandered off into the woods. Jannelle took the dog out but didn't stray more than ten feet from the porch, She heard a disturbance in the bushes next to the garden shed, grabbed Petunia and ran for the porch. Seconds after locking the door, she saw a figure, dressed all in black, step out of the shadows.

She couldn't see his face. He just stood there staring at her and not moving like he was trying to intimidate her. Instead of being afraid, she opened the door and stepped out on the porch, holding up her baseball bat in plain sight.

"I've called the police. You better beat feet if you know what's good for you," she yelled, waving her cell phone in the air. "I'm not afraid of you."

"You may not be, but your friend is. You didn't cancel the auction, so your friend will now pay for your stubbornness. Do you understand me?" he yelled back.

"If anything happens to Anita, I will hunt you down myself and you will pay the consequences. *Do* you understand me?"

"Stupid woman," he yelled as he ran back into the woods at the end of the property.

Jannelle returned to inside and called the station to report the incident. Chief Stanton happened to still be there going over the Paint and Sip phone records he had received from the phone company.

"The call came from a local number. Unfortunately, when we got to the house we found a closed up seasonal house with a smashed in back door. Because of the break-in we went inside looking for Anita, but no one was there, and it didn't look like anyone had been staying there either. I think whoever it was just broke in to use the phone," the chief stated.

"So that lead fizzled out," Jannelle replied. "If he used the house for a phone call, he could have Anita in any one of the vacant houses in the area."

"I called everyone in tomorrow morning and we will start to check all the closed houses in the area. It's all I can do for right now," the chief said.

"I'm stopping to visit with Mary in the morning before I go to work. I'll be at the Paint and Sip all day if you need to get a hold of me."

"Hopefully, we find Anita in one of the houses. Talk to you later."

Jannelle double-checked all the first-floor windows and doors to make sure they were all locked. She picked up Petunia and the bat and called for the cat to follow her upstairs. Once they were all in the bedroom, instead of putting up the gate the cat could jump over, Jannelle closed and locked the bedroom door. She felt safer keeping them all together in case the lunatic that took Anita decided to break into her house.

The rest of the night passed without incidence. Jannelle had slept through the night and when she unlocked the bedroom door, Picasso went running for the upstairs bathroom to use his litter box. Petunia watched him from the doorway and then followed the cat to the top of the stairs, waiting for Jannelle to pick her up and carry her downstairs.

After breakfast, they headed to town. Jannelle pulled into the rescue and noticed something strange going on in the parking lot. Everyone was standing out by their cars and not inside.

CHAPTER SIX

"What's going on?" Jannelle asked as she exited her car.

"There's some lunatic in there fighting with poor Mary, He started throwing things around, so we all took our animals and ran for safety," Mrs. Tome replied.

"Has anyone called the police?"

"Cindy did and she decided to stay inside in case Mary needed someone to help her."

"Do you know who it is?"

"Cindy said it was Mary's ex-fiancé."

"I'm going in. Please keep an eye on Picasso and Petunia for me," Jannelle said, heading for the rescue.

She opened the door and could hear the arguing coming from the office area. Cindy was standing outside the door, listening. She motioned for Jannelle to join her.

"I'm afraid he's going to hurt her," Cindy whispered. "I called the police."

"I told you it was over," they heard Mary yell.

"I'm going back to Boston, and you are coming with me. I promised a colleague you would run their animal hospital and I'm not going to look like a fool because you backed out on a promise I made. No one walks out on Brandon Boles. Do you understand me?"

"It's him," Jannelle muttered. "He took Anita."

"Are you sure?" Cindy asked.

"I finally can place where I knew the voice on the phone from. It's Brandon Boles."

"How long did the police say it would take them to get here?"

"They said they would be here in under ten minutes."

"We need to do something to keep him here. And I know what it is," she said, opening the door.

"Jannelle, you need to leave before you get hurt," Mary insisted through her tears.

"I'm not going anywhere. He's the one who took Anita, and I aim to find out where he hid her," Jannelle stated.

"You can't prove that" he snarled.

"I can…do you understand me?" Jannelle said, staring him down. "Is that the only phrase you know, Mr. Boles? You sure use it enough."

He glared at Jannelle.

"Is that true, Brandon? Did you kidnap Anita? How could you stoop so low as to do something like that?"

"He hoped if he stole the money meant for the x-ray machine and you couldn't get it, you would leave for a better equipped place to work. And when that didn't work, he insisted the auction be cancelled or he would harm Anita. Am I right, Mr. Boles?"

"Where is Anita, Brandon? Tell me right now," Mary demanded.

"I'm not telling you anything. This stupid woman can't prove a thing."

"Stupid woman. Isn't that what you called me last night when you were lurking outside my house making threats?" Jannelle asked, getting right in his face.

The sirens sounded in the distance and Boles knew he was in trouble if he didn't leave right then and there. He pushed Mary to the floor and went for Jannelle, but she was faster than he was, and she stuck her foot in between his ankles to trip him up. He fell to the floor and all three women pounced on top of him to hold him down.

The chief and two other deputies ran into the office, stopping short at the scene in front of them. Deputy Camp handcuffed him and pulled him to his feet.

"Take him to the station and book him for disturbing the peace and assault and battery on Mary," the chief ordered.

"Not yet," Jannelle replied. "He's the one who has Anita, and he wouldn't tell us where she was."

"Are you sure?" the chief asked.

"He won't tell us, but I think I just put two and two together and I think I know where Anita is," Jannelle stated.

"Where is she if you're so smart?" Boles taunted.

"Chief, if you send some of your men over to Karen Kramer's house, I think you will find Anita there."

Boles mouth dropped open.

When the chief saw the reaction of Boles to her statement, he radioed his deputies to go to Karen Kramer's house immediately. Boles shoulders slumped over, and he knew it was over.

"How did you figure this out?" the chief asked Jannelle.

"Several reasons. I thought it was strange she came into the store yesterday when she had never come anywhere near the place prior to that visit. She asked all kinds of questions about Anita and the auction and wanted to know if it had been cancelled. And not minutes after she left, I received the phone call telling me Anita would be hurt because I hadn't cancelled the auction like I was told to do. She had to have been the one who went to Boles and told him what was said."

"But why would Karen want the auction cancelled?" Mary asked.

"Because of the oldest reason on the books. Greed."

"Greed?"

"I had a visit yesterday from Carrie, Peter Kramer's stepsister. She told me that he was paying alimony to Karen and Carrie was also guarding the inheritance he was left from his dad. Karen has been trying to get the money since the divorce became final. She also told me that if either of them remarries, the alimony payments would stop, and Karen couldn't have that."

"What has that got to do with the rescue and the auction?" Mary asked.

"It doesn't have a lot to do with either, but has a lot to do with you, Mary," Jannelle answered.

"Me?"

Apparently, Peter had voiced an interest in dating you and word got back to Karen, and she needed you out of the picture. She couldn't have him dating anyone in case it developed into something more and she would lose her only income, the alimony. And if he remarried, she knew all shots at getting her hands on the inheritance would be out the window. How am I doing Mr. Boles?"

He growled and kept his eyes on the ground in front of him.

"If the auction fell through, Mr. Boles here figured Mary would return to Boston with him and take the job he promised someone she would take. The only part I haven't figured out is how they met and started working together," Jannelle said.

"How about it, Boles? Do you want to help yourself and tell us?" the chief asked the prisoner.

He stood there in silence.

"We have her! We found Anita and she's okay," a message from the chief's shoulder radio announced. "And we have Karen Kramer in custody."

"Bring her to the hospital and have her checked out. Make sure she's okay to go home," the chief ordered over the radio. "I'll call Sid and tell him to meet you there."

"Where is the money you stole from the rescue?" Mary demanded.

Silence.

"Get him out of here. We'll have a nice talk down at the station," the chief said, pushing Boles toward the deputies.

"Do you want the honor of calling Sid?" the chief asked Jannelle. "After all, it was you that figured out where she was."

"No, you make the call, please. I'll probably start crying and I don't want Sid thinking something has happened to her."

"Excuse me, then," he said, pulling out his personal cell phone.

"You know what the funny part is?" Mary asked. "I like Peter, too, but I could never tell anyone because I was engaged to Brandon. I knew he was a good man because of his love for animals and how well he took care of Pepper."

"Well, now there is nothing stopping you," Jannelle said, winking. "Or Peter."

"Cindy, would you be a dear and go out and tell the owners they can return inside now that the danger is over. We will be running behind schedule so if some of them want to reschedule, please accommodate their wishes," Mary requested.

"I'm going to the hospital to see my best friend. Opening the store will have to wait," Jannelle announced.

"I'm sure everyone will understand," Mary replied. "Thank you, Jannelle. For everything."

"The things we do for this rescue, I don't know," Jannelle said hugging the vet.

"Speaking of that, I do have a new senior cat I need a foster for," Mary said, smiling.

"Fine, if the cat gets along with Picasso and Petunia, you know I will not turn it away."

"I knew you wouldn't," Mary replied. "You're too full of love."

2 weeks later

The Paint and Sip was brimming over with people attending the auction. Anita was manning the wine selling table and couldn't keep up with the requests. Jannelle and the rest of the committee were walking around selling raffle tickets for the grand prize of the deck. An auction book had been printed up so the attendees could see what order the donations would be offered in.

Chief Stanton was going to be the auctioneer again and was walking around checking out the displayed items to familiarize himself with them. Millie jumped behind the table to help Anita catch up on the wine sales.

"What a great showing," the chief said to Jannelle. "The rescue is going to make out very well this year. And we recovered the stolen money at Karen's house, minus a few hundred, so the emergency and general fund should be in good shape for the upcoming year."

"I'm glad you recovered the money. Did you ever find out how Boles and Karen hooked up?"

"They both worked at the same bank up in Boston before she moved back home. They ran into each other at the diner and hatched the plan when they figured out they could both profit from working together."

"How was Boles going to profit from getting Mary to move to Boston?' Jannelle asked while handing someone a raffle ticket and collecting the money for it. "Thank you."

"Mary is one of the best vets in the region. There were three new animal hospitals that would be opening up in the Boston area and the company needed the outstanding reputation that Mary could provide. The owner promised Boles thirty thousand if he could get Mary to take the position."

"So, he really didn't care for Mary, he just wanted the money," Jannelle said, frowning.

"Sounds like it. But somehow I think she's over the whole ordeal," he said, looking behind her.

Jannelle looked in the direction of the door. Mary and Peter Kramer had just come through the door walking hand in hand. They looked so happy together. Jannelle was glad that Peter would never have to worry about his ex, ever again, and could have a happy life from here on out.

"I do believe you're right. The auction starts in ten minutes. Are you ready?"

"My teeth are glued in tightly and I am ready," he replied, laughing.

"Yeah, we wouldn't want a repeat of two years ago when your teeth came flying out and hit Mr. Peddles sitting in the front row."

"Believe me, that will never happen again. But it did make the front page of the paper, and I was famous for about three days," he replied. "Not in a good way, but famous just the same."

"Excuse me. I'm going to relieve Anita at the wine table so she can get the ball rolling and make all her necessary announcements. We have already hit the ten thousand mark but we won't know the full total until sometime next week after we finish collecting the money from the local businesses," Jannelle stated. "I can't wait to see who wins the deck."

Anita stepped to the front of the room and the loud chatter became a dull murmur. She made all the necessary announcements, thanked who needed to be thanked and then requested the big bushel basket that held all the raffle tickets bought in hopes to win the deck.

"Who wants to pick out the winning ticket?" she asked.

"I do," yelled a child from the back of the room.

"Step up here and pick a ticket," Anita told him.

He stuck his hand in the basket, swished the tickets around and came out with one ticket. He handed the winning ticket to Anita.

"Oh, dear, this is embarrassing," Anita said. "The winner is Sid Prowle, and the ticket was bought at the Denniston Hardware Store."

A cheer went up around the event. People stepped forward shaking Sid's hand and patting him on the back. Everyone seemed genuinely happy that he won.

"It couldn't have gone to someone who deserved it more after all they have been through," the chief said to Jannelle as he stepped up onto the platform next to the wine table to start the auction. "I love this town."

HOT AND BUBBLY TUNA TEASERS

Ingredients:

1-6 oz. can of tuna fish

I Tbsp. chili sauce or catsup

¼ tsp. Worcestershire sauce

¼ tsp. onion salt

¼ cup mayonnaise

2 Tbsp. any dry white wine

Flake tuna well with a fork. Blend in all the other ingredients. Spread on your favorite cracker or toast

HOT AND BUBBLY TUNA TEASERS

rounds. Sprinkle with paprika. Place on cookie sheets. Brown under broiler until hot and bubbly. Makes 18 to 20.

They are made quickly and gone just as fast.

FROSTED HAM BALLS

Ingredients:

½ pound cooked ham – ground or finely chopped

1/3 cup raisins

1 Tbsp. grated onion

¼ tsp. curry powder

¼ cup mayonnaise

1 3oz. package of cream cheese

1 Tbsp. milk

small amount of chopped parsley

FROSTED HAM BALLS

Mix first five ingredients and shape into a ball. Set on a serving plate and chill. Mix cream cheese with milk until smooth and then spread on chilled ball. Sprinkle with parsley and chill until serving time. Surround by crackers and serve. Makes about 2 cups.

MINI MAKE AHEAD QUICHES

Ingredients

1 package refrigerated butter flake dinner rolls (12)

1 4 ½ oz. can medium shrimp, drained

1 egg, beaten

½ cup light cream

1 Tbsp. brandy of choice

½ tsp. salt

6 slices of Swiss or Gruyere cheese

Grease 2 dozen 1 ¾ inch muffins pan. Separate each dinner roll in half and press into muffin tin to create shells. Place one shrimp in each shell. Combine egg, cream, brandy, salt and pepper. Divide the mixture evenly between shells. Cut the cheese slices into 4 slices each making a total of 24 triangles. Place one on top of each shell. Bake in a 375-degree oven for 20 minutes or until golden brown. Eat hot.

To save for another time…

Cool. Wrap in foil and freeze. To serve later on, place frozen appetizers on baking sheet. Bake at 375-degrees for 10 to 12 minutes.

STEAK POLYNESIAN

Ingredients:

6 cube steaks (about 1 ¼ pounds) 1/3 cup soy sauce

2 Tbsp. butter or margarine 3 Tbsp. brown sugar

¼ cup chopped onion and green pepper 1 tsp. ground ginger

½ tsp. salt 2 Tbsp. cornstarch

1/8 tsp. ground pepper 1/3 cup of cold water

1 can 14 oz. sliced pineapple with juice Hot cooked rice

STEAK POLYNESIAN

Brown steaks in butter or margarine in a large skillet. Add onion, green pepper, salt and pepper during the last half of browning. Add pineapple slices and the juice, soy sauce, brown sugar and ginger. Heat thoroughly. Blend cornstarch to a smooth paste with cold water.

Arrange meat, pineapple, onion and green pepper on a platter and keep warm. Stir cornstarch into the hot liquid left in the pan, cook, stirring constantly until sauce thickens and turns to clear. Pour over meat. Serve over a bed of hot rice. Serves 6

CONTACT DONNA CLANCY

You can find me on Facebook:

https://www.facebook.com/dwaloclancy/

or on my website:

https://www.donnaclancybooks.com/

or email me directly:

dwaloclancy@yahoo.com

Printed in Great Britain
by Amazon